This Book Belongs to:

UFO DIARY

First published in Great Britain in 1989 by Andersen Press Ltd., 20 Vauxhall Bridge Road, London SW1V 2SA.

This paperback edition first published in 2007 by Andersen Press Ltd.

Published in Australia by Random House Australia Pty., Level 3, 100 Pacific Highway, North Sydney, NSW 2060.

Copyright © Satoshi Kitamura, 1989.

Colour separated in Switzerland by Photolitho AG, Zürich. Printed and bound in Italy by Grafiche AZ, Verona.

10   9   8   7   6   5   4   3

British Library Cataloguing in Publication Data available.

ISBN 978 1 84270 591 9

This book has been printed on acid-free paper.

UFO DIARY

SATOSHI KITAMURA

ANDERSEN PRESS
LONDON

On Monday, I took a wrong turn in the Milky Way.

There in front of me was a strange blue planet,

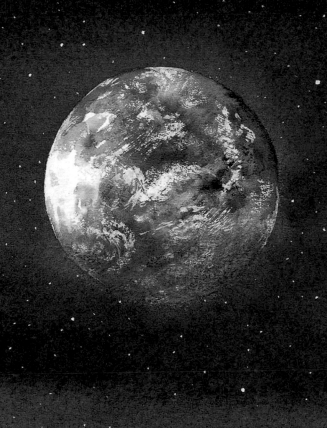

bright as a glass ball.

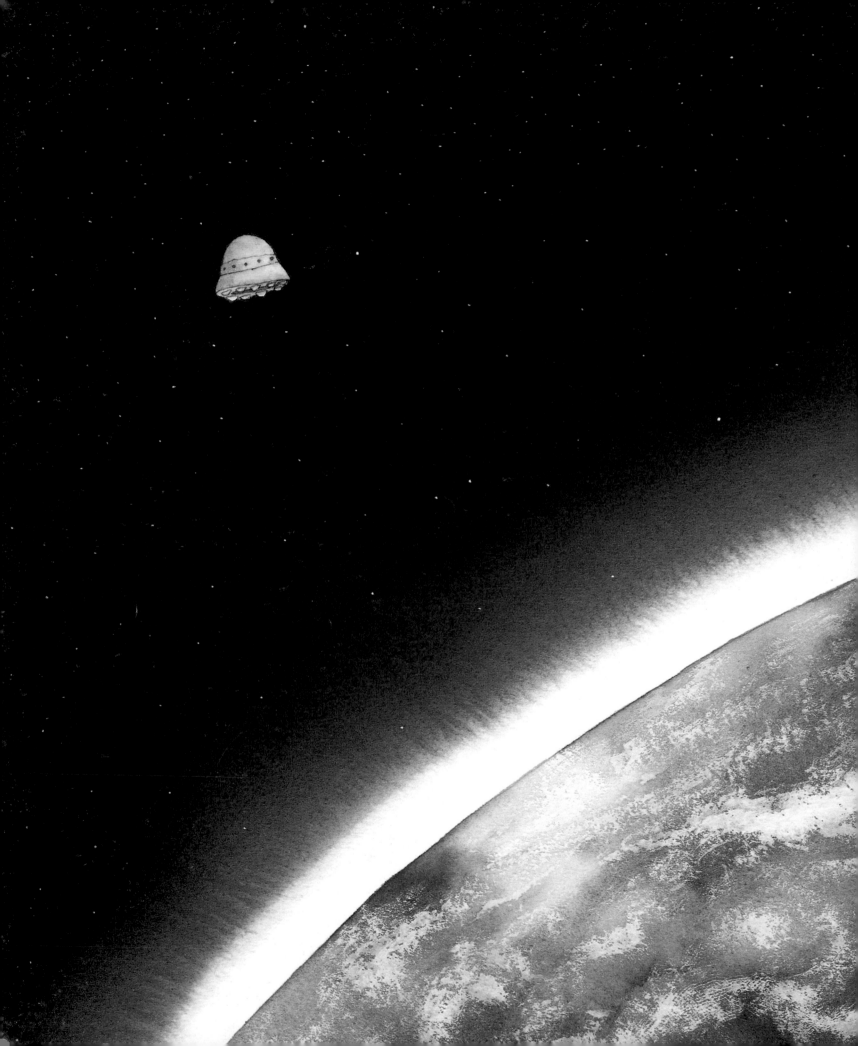

Between white clouds I saw shifting, changing patterns and

I flew on towards that patchwork of scattered islands and seas

until **I** saw a creature.

It stared at me as I landed.

What an odd-looking thing!

It spoke and I could not understand;
but I smiled. It smiled back.

Then I knew he was going to be my friend.

He showed me round and introduced me to his relations. We played for hours until it grew dark

and the sky lit up with a million constellations.
We looked up together and I showed him the way I had come.

There was the friendly light of my own planet.

It was time to go home;
but first he wanted to have a ride.

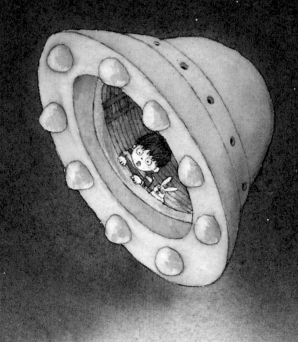

We whirled into the night,
spinning round his planet until he was giddy.

I dropped him home and he gave me a present.
It was yellow and grew in the field where we met.

"I'll plant it somewhere," I promised.
He smiled at me and we waved goodbye.

The planet slipped away beneath me.

It grew smaller and smaller

until at last it had vanished into the darkness of space.

Other titles by

SATOSHI KITAMURA

Angry Arthur (text by Hiawyn Oram)

In the Attic (text by Hiawyn Oram)

A Boy Wants a Dinosaur (text by Hiawyn Oram)

Ned and the Joybaloo (text by Hiawyn Oram)

Once Upon an Ordinary School Day (text by Colin McNaughton)

Comic Adventures of Boots

From Acorn to Zoo: and Everything in Between

Me and my Cat?

Pablo the Artist

Sheep in Wolves' Clothing

What's Inside?

When Sheep Cannot Sleep

Igor, The Bird Who Couldn't Sing